Breakfast at Danny's Diner

D0001605

By Judith Bauer Stamper
Illustrated by Chris Demarest

Grosset & Dunlap • New York

Chapter 1

It was 6:00 on a Saturday morning. The sun was just coming up. Tina, her twin brother, Tony, and their Uncle Danny got out of the car.

"Uncle Danny," Tina said. "When do you open the diner?"

"At 6:30," Danny said. "That's only a half-hour away. And we have lots of work to do!"

Tony yawned and rubbed his eyes. "But I'm still tired. I usually sleep late on Saturdays."

4

"Two of my workers called in sick,"
Danny said. "I'm lucky I have a niece and
nephew who can help out."

"I can't wait to work in the diner," Tina
said. "Come on, Tony, this is going to be
easy . . . a lot easier than going to school."

"You think working in a diner is easy?"
Uncle Danny asked with a smile. "We'll
see about that."

Danny unlocked the door. Tina and
Tony followed him inside.

"Your first job is to set up the tables,"
Uncle Danny said. "Count the tables and
booths. Then come into the kitchen."

"10 tables," Tony said.

"And 8 booths," Tina added. They ran
after Uncle Danny into the kitchen.

"Here are my place mats," Danny said.
"They show my special meals. Put 4 in
each booth. Put 2 on each table."

"I'll do the tables," Tony said. "2 place mats for 10 tables would be 2 plus 2 plus 2 . . ."

"Hey, we can use multiplication to figure it out," Tina said.

"Okay," Tony said. "10 tables with 2 place mats each would be 10 times 2. That equals . . . 20 place mats!"

Tony counted out 20 place mats and put them on the tables.

"8 booths times 4 place mats is . . ." Tina said. She started to go through the times tables for 8 in her head. "8 times 4 equals . . . 32," Tina said. She counted out 32 place mats and put down 4 in each booth.

"What should we do next?" Tina asked.

"Look at one of the place mats," Uncle Danny said. "There is a picture of my breakfast special. Everybody loves my special."

"3 eggs, any way you want them," Tony read, "with 4 sausages or 4 pieces of bacon."

"2 pieces of toast, white or whole-wheat," Tina added. "Plus, juice, milk, tea, or coffee."

"Wow, that's a great special!" Tony said.

"You bet it is," Uncle Danny said. "You kids are going to be in the kitchen helping Angelo, the cook. When an order comes in, you will get the food ready for him."

"Okay, Tony, how many eggs do you need for 3 Danny's specials?" Uncle Danny asked.

"Uh, 3 eggs times 3 orders would be . . ." Tony stopped to think.

"3 sets of 3 equals 9 eggs!" Tina filled in.

"Hey," Tony said, "I wanted to figure that out!"

"How many sausages would you need for 4 of my specials?" Danny asked.

"4 sausages times 4 specials would be—" Tina began.

"16 sausages!" Tony yelled.

Just then, the back door of the diner opened. A man walked in carrying 2 big bags.

"Hey, Carlos, good to see you," Danny said.

"2 dozen bagels. 2 dozen doughnuts," Carlos said as he set the bags on the table. "And 2 extra of each. Have a good day!"

11

Tina started to figure out how many bagels and doughnuts there were.

"A dozen is 12," she said. And, 2 times 12 is 24. Plus 2 extra makes 26 of each."

"Bagels and doughnuts. Yum!" Tony said.

"Eat one, if you want," Uncle Danny said. "Then stack them in the glass cases on the counter outside. And make sure the stacks are equal."

Uncle Danny went out into the diner to start the coffee. Tony grabbed a big raisin bagel. Tina ate a doughnut.

"We'd better eat a lot," Tony said. "For energy."

"Want to split a doughnut?" Tina asked.

"Sure!" Tony said, reaching for the half she gave him.

"Kids!" Uncle Danny called. "It's 6:20. We open in 10 minutes."

Tony and Tina jumped up and carried the bags into the diner.

"There were 26 doughnuts," Tina said. "And between you and I, we ate 2. So that leaves 24. 4 doughnuts in a stack looks just right. So how many stacks of 4 do we need?

"What number times 4 equals 24?" Tony asked.

"5 times 4 is 20 . . ." Tina said. "6 times 4 is 24! We'll make 6 equal stacks of 4 doughnuts each."

"What about the bagels?" Tony asked Tina. He started to make stacks of 4 bagels each.

"Uh-oh," he said. "There's one bagel left. Where should we put it?"

"Why don't we just eat it?" Tina said.

"But I'm too full," Tony moaned.

Tina tore the bagel in half and stuffed half of it in her mouth. She gave the other half to Tony.

"Get ready, kids," Danny called from the kitchen. "It's 6:27. Danny's Diner opens in 3 minutes!"

Chapter Two

Tony and Tina rushed into the kitchen.

"Meet Angelo, my short-order cook,"
Uncle Danny said. "Angelo, this is Tony
and Tina."

"Hi kids," Angelo said. "Danny tells me
you're helping me cook this morning."

"Yep," Tony said. He rubbed his
stomach, which didn't feel too good.

17

"Wash your hands, kids," Uncle Danny said. "Then put on these aprons."

Tina and Tony got ready to help in the kitchen. Then they walked over to Angelo.

"When an order comes in, it goes on a clip in front of the stove," Angelo said. "I'll yell out what the order is. You set up the things I need."

"Uncle Danny told us," Tina said. "It seems easy."

"Easy? We'll see about that," Angelo said.

Just then the front door of the diner swung open. A woman in a waitress uniform rushed in.

"Teresa, am I glad to see you!" Danny said. "We're missing Mary and Luis this morning. My niece and nephew, Tina and Tony, are helping out."

"This is going to be some day!" Teresa said. "And here come the first customers!"

6 people walked into the diner. 2 sat at a table. The other 4 took a booth.

"Good morning," Danny called out to them.

Teresa rushed over to take their orders.

"Open up the cartons of eggs," Angelo told Tina. "Tony, you're in charge of making toast."

Teresa came up to the open window between the kitchen and the dining room. She clipped on 2 orders. Angelo gave them a quick look.

"6 Danny's specials," he called out. "2 with sausage, 4 with bacon, 4 with white toast, 2 with whole-wheat."

Tina stared at the egg cartons. There were 6 orders. Each order needed 3 eggs. She remembered her multiplication tables. 6 times 3 is . . . 18.

Tina took all the eggs out of 1 carton and put them on the egg tray by the stove . . . that was 12. Then she took 6 eggs out of another carton. That made 18.

"Always put out the sausage and bacon first," Angelo said. "I start that before the eggs."

Tina started to get nervous. There was so much to remember and so much to figure out. It was all happening so fast!

Each Danny's special had 4 sausages or 4 pieces of bacon. So, 2 orders times 4 sausages would be . . . 8 sausages. And, 4 orders times 4 pieces of bacon would be . . .

Angelo interrupted her thinking. "8 sausages and 16 pieces of bacon," he said.

Tina quickly counted out the sausages and bacon. Angelo started to cook. Soon, sausages, bacon, and eggs were sizzling on the grill.

Tony reached for the bread. 4 orders times 2 slices of white toast equaled 8 slices of white bread. 2 orders of 2 slices of wheat toast equaled 4 slices of wheat bread. Tony put the bread in the big toaster.

The toast popped up just as Angelo put the eggs, bacon, and sausages on 6 plates. Tony added the toast. Just then, Teresa clipped on 3 more orders. She picked up the plates full of food and rushed to deliver them.

Angelo looked at the new orders.

"1 special with sausage and white," he called out. "2 stacks of blueberry pancakes."

Tina's eyes got wide. Pancakes?

"Tony, you get the special ready and take care of the toast." Angelo said. "Tina, I'll show you how to mix up the pancake batter."

Tina started to get nervous. She accidentally knocked over an egg carton. Two eggs splattered on her face and apron.

"Oh, no!" Tina said. She wiped the eggs off the table with a paper towel.

"Don't cry over spilled eggs," Angelo said. "Let's get to work on the pancakes."

Angelo set out a big bowl on the worktable. Next, he set out flour, eggs, milk, and butter.

"Okay, Tina," Angelo said, "Making pancakes is simple. Here's the recipe:

2 eggs   2 cups flour

4 pats butter   1 cup blueberries

1 cup milk

"First, you beat the eggs, butter, and milk together. Next, you stir in the flour. Then, you add the blueberries."

Tina took a deep breath and got to work. She mixed together the eggs, butter, and milk. Next she put in the flour mixture. A puff of flour flew up into her face.

"Tina, you look like a ghost!" Tony said, laughing.

Tina laughed, and wiped the flour off her face. Then she stirred up the pancake mixture and added the blueberries. Her arm started to ache from beating the batter.

"Is it ready?" she asked Angelo, showing him the bowl.

"Perfect," Angelo said. He took the bowl over to the stove and spooned the batter onto the griddle. The pancakes began to brown and bubble.

Angelo flipped the cakes over to brown on the other side. Then he flipped them onto the plates, 6 pancakes in a stack. Teresa ran up and whisked the plates away.

When Teresa came back, she didn't look happy.

"Angelo, we're in big trouble," she said.

"What's the matter, Teresa?" Angelo asked.

"Look outside the window," Teresa said.

Tony and Tina stood on their tiptoes
to look out. A big yellow school bus was
sitting in the parking lot. And, just then,
the door to Danny's Diner swung open.

A crowd of kids burst into the diner.
They were wearing baseball uniforms.

"It's our school's baseball team!" Tony
said.

"How will we ever feed them all?"
Teresa said with a moan.

Chapter Three

Tony and Tina watched as the baseball team filled up the tables and booths.

"Tina, isn't that your teacher, Mr. Lewis?" Tony asked.

"Yes! He's the school's baseball coach, too," Tina explained.

Uncle Danny came running into the kitchen. "Every booth and table is full. What a day. What a day!"

Tony was busy counting the number of kids.

"There are 15 kids plus Mr. Lewis," he said. "What if they all order something different?"

"We'll find out soon," Teresa said. She walked to the booths to take their orders.

"Angelo," Tina asked. "What's the easiest thing for you to make in big amounts?"

Angelo scratched his head. Then he answered. "Pancakes. Pancakes are easy . . . if I have somebody to help me mix them up."

Tina wiped her hands on her apron and headed for the kitchen door.

"I'll be right back," she said. Then she walked over to the booths where the baseball team was busy studying their menus..

"Hey, check out Danny's special," one boy said.

"It looks good. But Coach Lewis doesn't like us to eat sausages or bacon before a game," a girl added.

"I know what I want," another player said, "a doughnut."

"A doughnut won't give you enough energy," Coach Lewis said. "We've got a big game ahead of us today."

Tina walked up to the booth where
Coach Lewis was sitting with 3 players.

"Hi, Mr. Lewis," she said.

"Tina, what are you doing here?" Mr.
Lewis asked.

Teresa spoke up. "She's helping her
Uncle Danny. We're a little short-handed
here this morning."

"I know something that everybody would like to eat," Tina said. "And it's great for energy."

"What is it, Tina?" Mr. Lewis said.

"First, you could all start with a glass of orange juice," Tina said. "Then, you could eat Danny's delicious blueberry pancakes."

"Blueberry pancakes," one boy said. "Cool!"

"How about it team?" Mr. Lewis asked.

"Yeah, blueberry pancakes," everybody shouted.

Teresa let out a sigh of relief. She wrote down the order and repeated it aloud. "16 glasses of orange juice. 16 stacks of blueberry pancakes. Coming right up!"

Tina ran back to the kitchen. She rushed over to the worktable.

Teresa clipped the order above Angelo's stove.

"16 stacks of blueberry pancakes," he
read aloud. "Start mixing, Tina! Tony, you
help Teresa pour the glasses of orange
juice!"

"Is it okay if I make 2 batches at a time?"
Tina asked.

"That's the only way we'll ever get these
pancakes made!" Angelo said.

2×2 eggs $= 4$ eggs
2×4 pats of butter $= 8$ pats
2×1 cup of milk $= 2$ cups
2×2 cups of flour $= 4$ cups
2×1 cup of blueberries $= 2$ cups

Tina looked at the pancake recipe. "How can I double this recipe?" she thought out loud. "I need to multiply all of the ingredients by 2. That way, there will be twice the amount of batter. 2 times 2 eggs is 4 eggs. 2 times 4 pats of butter is 8 pats of butter. 2 times 1 cup of milk is 2 cups of milk. 2 times 2 cups of flour is 4 cups of flour. And 2 times 1 cup of blueberries is 2 cups of blueberries."

First, Tina beat together the eggs, butter, and milk. Next, she added the flour. At the end, she added the blueberries. Her arm was aching, but she kept mixing.

"First batch of pancake mix, coming up," Tina said.

"Good job, Tina," Angelo said. "Go ahead and start another batch."

Tina measured and mixed and measured and mixed. The pancakes sizzled on the grill. Angelo flipped them onto plates. Teresa came and whisked the plates away.

"14, 15, 16!" Angelo said as he dished up the last stacks of pancakes. "That does it!"

Tina sank down onto a stool in front of the worktable. She had never worked so hard in her life! And she never wanted to see another blueberry pancake for as long as she lived.

Uncle Danny came into the kitchen.

"Good thinking, Tina," he said. "You saved the day at Danny's Diner!"

"Thanks, Uncle Danny," Tina said. "But I was wrong about something. Working in a diner isn't easy. And it has even more math than school!"

Uncle Danny didn't say a thing. But he had a big smile on his face.

Teresa came into the kitchen and plopped down on a stool. "Rush hour is over!" she said, rolling her eyes.

"Kids, it's time you took a break," Uncle Danny said. "Go out and sit in the empty booth and relax."

Tony and Tina staggered out of the kitchen and slid into the empty booth.

"I'm so tired," Tina said with a yawn.

"I'm so full," Tony added. "I'll never eat again!"

"Me, neither!" Tina said. She looked over at Tony. His head was resting on the back of the booth. And his eyes were closed.

Tony and Tina opened their eyes. Slowly, their eyes got bigger and bigger. Sitting in front of each of them was a high stack of blueberry pancakes.

"You two deserve a reward for your hard work," Uncle Danny said with a smile. "Breakfast at Danny's Diner!"